Contents

How COOL are the Jedi?   6

Did someone say... **Jedi?**   20

The great and the good   48

Trial and (T)error   88

We need another hero   110

Glossary   124

Index   126

Acknowledgements   128

HOW COOL ARE THE

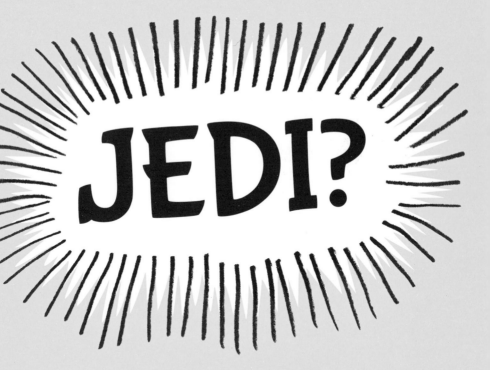

JEDI?

So you want to know **what it takes** to walk the Jedi path?

Excellent question.

It's not for the faint of heart. Becoming one of the guardians of **peace and justice** in the galaxy requires courage, patience, and dedication.

Okay, they're in the air... now what?

It's not all just swinging a lightsaber around, **lifting rocks** with your mind, and waving your hand in front of a stormtrooper to escape their clutches.

Being a Jedi means **following in the footsteps** of a thousand generations of Jedi. That's a lot of pressure. And you can bet there are a lot of ⓇⓊⓁⒺⓈ, too!

On the other hand, being a Jedi is ⓐⓦⒺⓈⓄⓂⒺ. Jedi get to travel across the galaxy (sometimes at **LIGHTSPEED**) and defend the innocent. And obviously, they have *lightsabers.*

So come on, let's discover the mysterious and wonderful world... of the JEDI.

A QUICK HISTORY LESSON:

According to legend, the Jedi Order began before there was any sort of system or government in the galaxy. The aim of this ancient gang of good guys was **to keep the galaxy a peaceful, happy place.** But we all know that things don't always go according to plan. Dun dun dunnn!

Over the years, the Jedi have faced many difficult times, but they have **never given up.**

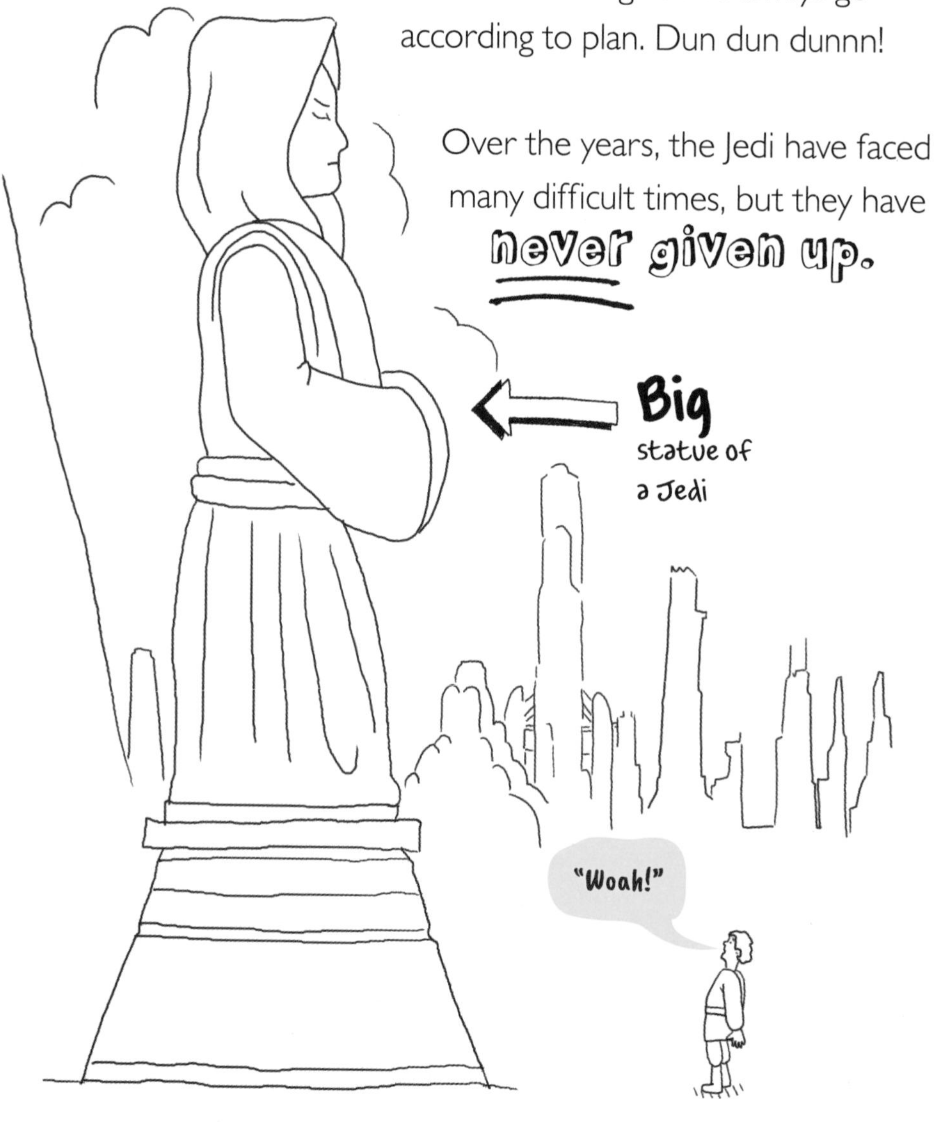

← **Big** statue of a Jedi

"Woah!"

That's how their legacy continues to endure. The Jedi are wise. Everybody knows that. But no one's perfect. No one. Actually, the wisest Jedi of all are those who realize it's important to **LEARN FROM FAILURE AND GROW FROM IT.** After some learning and growing, a Jedi can become a **great warrior,** a **renowned peacekeeper,** a **hero,** and even a

legend!

Jedi pass their knowledge down from Jedi Master to Padawan learner. Jedi knowledge also comes from **experience,** not just the **Sacred Jedi Texts.**

Good thing too, because as a great Jedi Master once said:

Page turners they were not.*

Jedi texts:
Ancient – yes
Sacred – yes
Interesting – Ummm...

*It was Yoda who said this.

11

They **make peace** between people at war, negotiate treaties, undertake **daring secret missions,** and work as bodyguards, spies, couriers, scientists, and even, during the Clone Wars, as generals. Unfortunately, "taking it easy" is not part of a Jedi's life.

It's such a tough job that training to be a Jedi begins in **early childhood.** If this makes you wonder about Luke Skywalker, who only learned he was a Jedi at age 19, you should know that he was really, **REALLY** late to the party.

Traditionally, **Force-sensitive** children leave home at a very young age (we're talking just four or five years old) to begin their Jedi training. They become Jedi **Younglings.**

I want to be a general.

I want to be a spy.

I just wanted to be a speeder truck driver!

As younglings grow up, they look toward completing their Jedi training. The first step is to **find a mentor.** Preferably a wise mentor who recognizes potential in a promising youngster – and takes a leap of faith to train them.

Finding Anakin was my destiny. He WILL bring balance to the Force.

We love you Qui-Gon!

Someone like Qui-Gon Jinn. He saw the potential of a young boy called Anakin Skywalker.

Qui-Gon realised that Anakin had an **amazing Force connection** and he refused to stop going on about it until Anakin was **approved** as a new Jedi recruit.

Blah, blah, blah, blah, blah, blah, blah, Anakin, blah, blah, destiny, blah, blah, blah, The Force, blah, blah, blah, blah, blah, blah, Anakin, blah, blah, blah, blah, blah, blah, Anakin, blah, blah, blah, Anakin, blah, blah, blah, blah, blah, blah, blah, blah...

Okay, maybe he didn't realise how **dangerous** someone as powerful as Anakin could be, but he gave a kid a chance. We **ALL** need someone to **give us a chance,** right?

Young Anakin Skywalker was given a chance, all right. One second he's a 𝕤𝕝𝕒𝕧𝕖 on the dusty, out-of-the-way planet Tatooine, and the next he's living on Coruscant, the capital of the galaxy, and **training to be a Jedi.**

I'll balance the Force all right. Now, which way shall I go?

LIGHT SIDE

DARK SIDE

Anakin
(age 9)

As a Jedi grows up, it becomes clear that everyone has a unique destiny in the Force.

But only you  can find your own path.

Will you follow the Jedi guidelines and pursue the **light side** of the Force? Will you try to reach the rank of Jedi Master and **become a mentor** to your own youngling? Will you make decisions that change

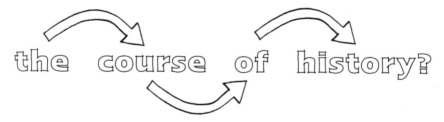

the course of history?

Or will you be tempted by the power of the **DARK SIDE?** Trust me, that's not the way you want to go…

So let's spare a thought for all those Jedi hopefuls out there. They're probably only just realising that it's not all about **mind tricks** and **clashing lightsabers** with Sith Lords.

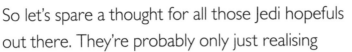

Easy mate!

It's also not about sending battle droids flying through the air with **A WAVE OF YOUR HAND** or piloting starfighters with lightning reflexes.

Hmmm... guess I'll wear brown again today!

It's about **focus, self-discipline,** and a closet full of identical robes for every occasion. Plus a healthy **sense of humour** to get through all the training ahead.

Let's salute the **younglings** who are ready to be challenged. When they fail to block that blaster bolt from a training remote, the only move they have left is to **laugh it off** – and try again.

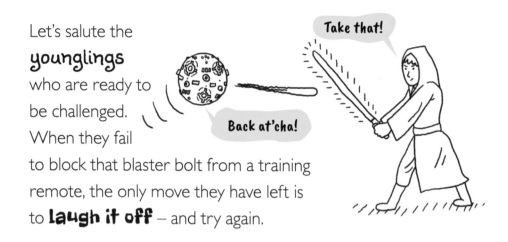

Getting back up after you've been knocked down shows you're truly cut out to be a Jedi.

That's exactly the sort of person the **galaxy** wants in its **HOUR OF GREATEST NEED.**

What is a Jedi?

"Hello there! I'm a Jedi."

Hooded Jedi cloak

Utility belt (including comlink, homing beacon, and other cool gadgets)

Lightsaber (don't hold it the wrong way)

Loose fabric to allow for movement

Sturdy boots

The Jedi are guardians of **peace** and **justice.** They travel the galaxy resolving disputes, ending conflicts, battling injustice, and showing off some pretty **MIND-BLOWING** skills. They do all of this — and pursue knowledge and wisdom — by studying

the FORCE.

As long as a person has a strong connection with the Force, they can learn to become a Jedi. **It doesn't matter** if you are small and green with oversize ears, or if you have tails growing out of your head — or even if you have a neck that is

t h r e e   f e e t   l o n g.

The Jedi are super respected across the galaxy (except by their enemies, obviously). On a few truly far, far away planets, the **legends of the Jedi** are so epic, some people don't even believe they exist*.

*But they do.

The Jedi Order

No one knows exactly when the Jedi Order began, just that it was quite a while ago and that it's been going on for

a <u>thousand</u> generations.

(Yes, that's a very, very long time!) The Order organises all the Jedi across the galaxy, finds and trains new Jedi, and works to **pursue peace and justice** for everyone.

An awesome organisation needs an awesome symbol!

Jedi Order symbol
Following the light side of the Force not only sounds cool, but it's a fitting phrase because light side devotees think that all people are luminous beings. And that's why the symbol of the Jedi Order looks like a starburst. Obviously.

Jedi can be found all over the place. Usually, they're on a mission to **protect** or **locate** something, although sometimes they're in exile on a remote planet. Either way, the Jedi really rack up those frequent-flyer parsecs!

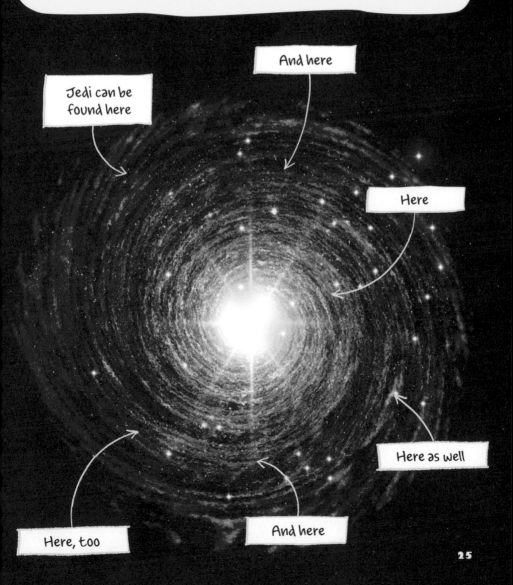

And here

Jedi can be found here

Here

Here as well

Here, too

And here

Now here's a question everyone likes to ask:

what, oh what, is the Force?

Well…

An **energy field** generated by all life, the Force is.

Surrounds and **connects all beings** to one another, the Force does.

Know why we are talking **backwards,** we do not.

The Force exists **everywhere**

across the galaxy where there is **life.** It is energy created by all living things. If you think that sounds very **hand-wavy** and **mystical,** you'd be right! But it is what it is. Some people are sensitive to the Force, and can even control it. These lucky ducks are known as **FORCE SENSITIVES,** and they have the potential to train in the ways of the Jedi.

The Force is strong
with this one. ——————➤

Force Sensitives are pretty cool: they can use the Force to **move objects _with their minds,_** have enhanced reflexes, sense things that are going on somewhere else, and employ mind tricks.

←——— These are just wavy
lines. You can't
see the real Force,
because it's invisible.

Hey! Who keeps
moving my stuff?

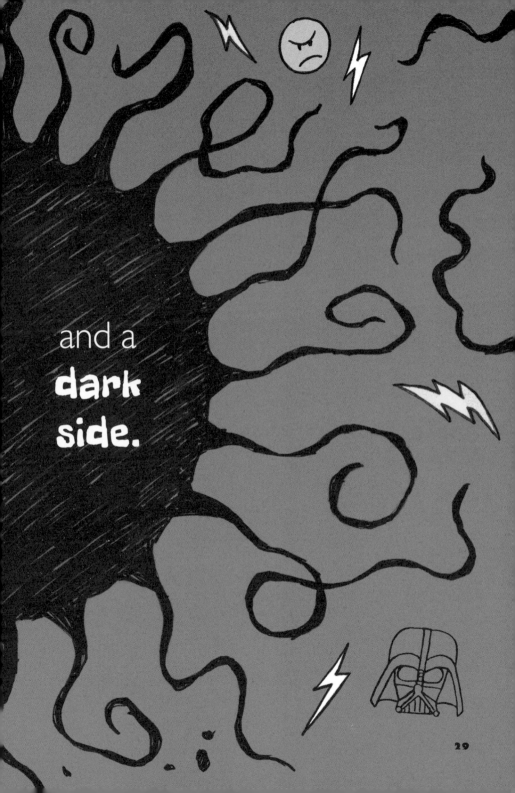

and a
**dark
side.**

29

The light side of the Force is peaceful. It's all about **connecting** to life around you and **listening** to what the universe is telling you. The dark side is a little bit more...

It's about **power** and learning to **control** others. From what I can tell, it's exhausting and will leave you bitter, miserable, with **yellow eyes,**

and with your first name changed to Darth. Avoid it!

I think Darth is quite a nice name, actually!

The three pillars of the Jedi Code. Okay, they're not LITERALLY pillars, but can you see what I did there?!

The Jedi Order follows a code that helps master the light side of the Force. The code is built around **three pillars of thought** that the Jedi like to meditate on:

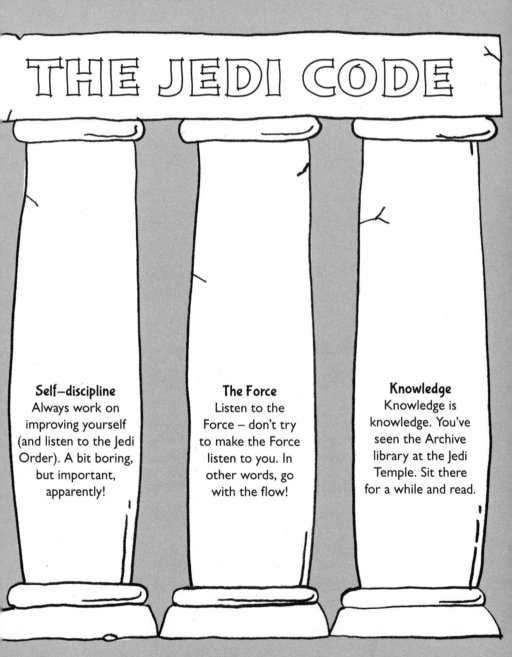

THE JEDI CODE

Self-discipline
Always work on improving yourself (and listen to the Jedi Order). A bit boring, but important, apparently!

The Force
Listen to the Force – don't try to make the Force listen to you. In other words, go with the flow!

Knowledge
Knowledge is knowledge. You've seen the Archive library at the Jedi Temple. Sit there for a while and read.

The light side of the Force is invisible, but if it wasn't, it would probably look like this: white, bright, and shiny.

TIME TO LOOK ON THE LIGHT SIDE:

This part's pretty easy to remember – the good guys follow the **light side** of the Force, while the baddies follow the **dark side.** But what **IS** the light side?

JUSTICE

INNER STRENGTH

FAIRNESS

Here's a mantra from the **Jedi Code** to help explain things:

> THERE IS NO EMOTION, THERE IS peace.
>
> THERE IS NO IGNORANCE, THERE IS knowledge.
>
> THERE IS NO PASSION, THERE IS serenity.
>
> THERE IS NO CHAOS, THERE IS harmony.
>
> THERE IS NO DEATH, THERE IS the Force.

Deep, right?

Okay, okay, the mantra is **AWESOME** and super philosophical, but it's **NOT EXACTLY CLEAR.** So here's a handy note for you:

Light side =
peace
+
calm
+
harmony
+
awareness

Think **meditation.** Think **nature.** Think **zen...**

Let's be honest. The light side sounds a bit **hard to put into practice,** doesn't it? Being one with the Force, connecting to all living beings. Finding **Serenity.**

BUT WAIT!

Let's break it down in more practical terms:
A light side user feels **connected to every being** around them, even when they're battling one of them – for example, a rampaging acklay beast. It is **this connection** that allows a Jedi to **anticipate** an opponent's attacks.

Terrible danger (a.k.a. an acklay)

The light side way: calm optimism, even in the face of terrible danger.

Here's an important fact: light siders use the Force for **defence,** never for **attack.** If that acklay would just mind its own business, the Jedi would leave it alone!

THE LIGHT SIDER'S PRACTICAL GUIDE TO LIFE:

* Try listening more than you talk.
* Understand that you'll **never** be totally in control.
* Open yourself up to the world around you.
* Live in the moment, without obsessing about living in the moment.
* **BE LOYAL** to your friends, but don't be afraid to let them go.

In other words,
not everything is about you!
(Remember that and you're good to go.)

The Dark Side

Sorry to say, the Jedi are not the only Force users in the galaxy. If you see someone with a red lightsaber, yellow eyes, face tattoos or a mask, and an affinity for **all-black clothing,** that person might have turned to the dark side. You'll need to know these guys, they're called the **SITH.**

PASSION!

The only thing dark siders have in common with the Jedi is their love of **hoods.** The Jedi believe in using their power for **good,** but the dark side is about channelling a Force user's **FEAR** or **RAGE.** Their fear leads them to anger and hatred and, finally, suffering. Which means they're not very fun to be around. Inside, they are pretty unhappy, too. You can tell by their **glum, cross** faces!

Fear of losing the things he loved drove Jedi **Anakin Skywalker** to embrace the dark side and become

DARTH VADER.

In truth, Vader didn't look much happier when he was a Jedi!

Anger, hatred, resentment, and a desire for power drove **DARTH MAUL, KYLO REN,** and the mysterious **SNOKE,** too. Turning to the dark side gave them power, but at a price.

Darth Vader

Think of this: when you're **really mad,** sometimes you feel more energetic, right? Like you might want to run around and scream and shout. Or even **THROW THINGS.** But it's not good energy (Yoda says to please stop throwing things). You wouldn't want to feel like that all the time; you'd tire yourself out!

Super cross

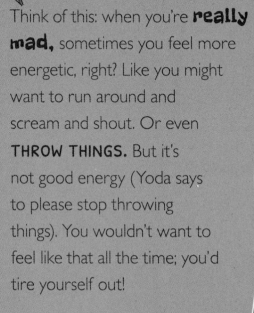

Emperor Palpatine

Never a smile

But to the followers of the dark side, short **bursts of anger** can cause them to do things like conjure Force lightning, or try to take over the galaxy.

Darth Maul

I used to be a Jedi, you know!

Count Dooku was a Jedi Master, trained by Yoda himself. Until he turned to the dark side.

There comes a time when every Force user must **make a choice.** Will they walk the path of **LIGHT** and be in harmony with everything around them? Or will they choose the **dark side** and pursue control and order, no matter the price?

And the choice between light and dark isn't as simple as you might think: plenty of Jedi have **turned** to the dark side. Very few have returned from it.

Me, too!

Darth Vader

Me three!

Pong Krell

And me... sort of.

Kylo Ren

Even well-meaning light siders can act in service to the dark side **WITHOUT KNOWING IT** (oops!). For example, when the Jedi became generals instead of peacekeepers during the Clone Wars. They waged **war** on behalf of the Republic, but actually they were walking right into Darth Sidious's **ultimate Jedi trap.** The clone troopers turned against them and wiped most of them out.

So choose **wisely!** Make sure you're not just doing the right thing — but the right thing for the **right** reasons.

Ta-da! your search for the Chosen One is over. Oh, wait a minute...

The Jedi have an ancient prophecy about the so-called **chosen one.** We all know someone who thinks **they** are the chosen one, but I'm talking about a **Jedi prophecy** here, not some big-headed kid in your class.

Now remember this: **THE LIGHT SIDE AND THE DARK SIDE ARE MEANT TO BE IN BALANCE.** The Chosen One is the Force user who will supposedly bring about that balance.

Aargh, this is harder than it looks!

The Jedi thought Anakin Skywalker was the Chosen One because he was **the most Force-sensitive person** they'd ever encountered. But then he turned to the dark side and became Darth Vader*.

*Booooo!

Go Anakin!

13 years later...

BUT...

Maybe Anakin becoming the terrifying Sith Lord Darth Vader **was** balancing the Force? Hmmm, but also maybe not since the galaxy was **plunged into darkness** and the Jedi were hunted down after that. But then, Anakin became good again and defeated the Emperor. So he did bring balance at some point. Maybe he **WAS** the Chosen One after all?

Wow... now I'm REALLY confused!

As you can see, this Chosen One business is exciting, but can **never fully be resolved** because the light and dark sides can never stay fully in balance. Someone will always try to defeat the other and the scales will tip all over again. **Still, it makes for a good story.**

Now that you've learned all about the Force, here's an extra factoid, just to make things more interesting.

There are actually **TWO** dimensions to the Force: the Living Force generated by all life (about which we are now experts) and the COSMIC FORCE that exists on its own throughout the galaxy.

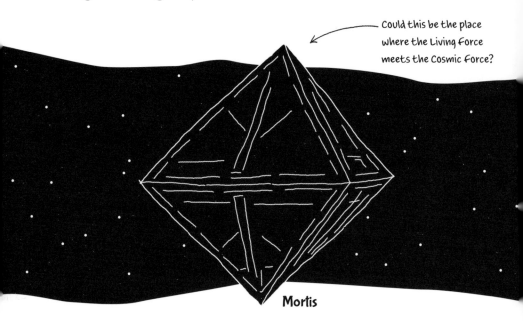

Could this be the place where the Living Force meets the Cosmic Force?

Mortis

There are certain places in the galaxy where the Cosmic Force is especially strong. The Jedi temple on Lothal was built over a **Force portal,** and Darth Vader built his temple over an **ancient well** of Force energy on Mustafar. Legend has it that the Living Force feeds into the Cosmic Force at a special realm called **MORTIS,** which exists outside of time and space.

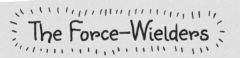

The Force-Wielders

Mortis is a strange place, home to three (very strange) beings, known as the Force-Wielders:

The Daughter
Full of power to create
and renew. Represents
the light side.

The Father
Keeps his two children in
balance – one cannot
exist without the other.

The Son
Prone to unleashing
chaos and destruction.
Yep, he's dark side.

There are rumours that these three can keep
the Force in balance throughout the galaxy.

The GREAT and the GOOD

Ki-Adi-Mundi

Adi Gallia

Shaak Ti

Even Piell

Plo Koon

Saesee Tiin

There are more than 10,000 Jedi across the galaxy negotiating (slightly boring) **trade disputes,** stopping cantina **brawls,** protecting planets, **AVOIDING WARS,** and *duelling* deadly Sith warriors. But who is in charge?

Introducing…

the Jedi High Council!

Made up of twelve of the **wisest** and **most experienced** Jedi Masters. They oversee the entire Jedi Order and basically boss all the other Jedi around, in a good way.

Oppo Rancisis

Eeth Koth

Yoda

Mace Windu

Depa Billaba

Coleman Trebor

The Jedi High Council meets in the council chamber, which, coincidentally, is very **HIGH.** It's located at the top of one of the four towers of the Jedi Temple on Coruscant, the capital of the whole galaxy. I guess high rank comes with a **great view.**

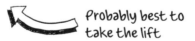

Probably best to take the lift

The leader of the High Council is called the **GRAND MASTER.** Yoda is one of the greatest, or shall we say grandest, Grand Masters in galactic history.

With such an impressive and vast history, the Jedi Order needs an **impressively vast** building, right? Enter the Jedi Temple on Coruscant, the main Jedi HQ. It's big. Very big. It's also located close to the Senate building to show just how

IMPORTANT

the Jedi are considered to be.

The Temple is built in the style of a ziggurat (sort of like a square-ish pyramid). Inside, there are **thousands of rooms:** classrooms, briefing rooms, map rooms, council chambers, meditation rooms, archives, and hangars – even a large **INDOOR GARDEN** for when Jedi want to meditate, called the **Room of a Thousand Fountains.** You'd better have a clear connection to the Force – or a really good map! – to avoid getting lost in here.

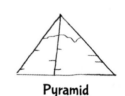

Pyramid

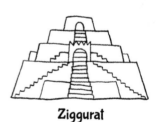

Ziggurat

Do you want to go **DEEPER** into the
JEDI TEMPLE and learn some Jedi secrets?

YES!

Over the centuries, the Jedi have accumulated a **lot**
of knowledge. That's like more knowledge than any
one Jedi could possibly learn in their **lifetime.**

The Jedi Archives are housed in the Jedi Temple.
We're not talking about shelves of books and paper (duh!) –

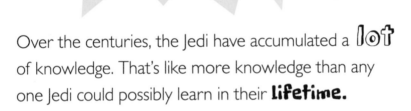

think **glowing data tablets,**
crammed with lore about mysteries of the
Force, sects that splintered off from the
main Jedi Order, secret lightsaber techniques,*
and so much more.

Shhhhh! This
is a library!

*Ooooh!

Jedi librarian, Jocasta Nu

So. Much. Data.

But who has time to learn all that? Not you? Is that why you're reading this book instead? Okay, so my advice is to seek out **holocrons.** These are precious **memory cubes** from **actual** Jedi. This means that even long-dead Jedi can tell you their stories and secrets.

Jedi holocron

Do **NOT** lose this

Here's some more **SECRET Jedi history** for you:
The very earliest Jedi studied on a small,
rainswept island on the ocean planet of **Ahch-To.**
There was one particularly gifted Force user who built
the very first **JEDI TEMPLE** here.

Luke was here.
(He hid on
Ahch-To during
his exile.)

All that's left of the ancient
Jedi who studied here (apart
from simple huts) is a mosaic
of the Prime Jedi and a few
dusty old Jedi books.

Unfortunately (and quite strangely), **nobody** can **remember** who this gifted Force user was, so everyone just calls them the

Prime Jedi.

Ancient mosaic

Stone hut

So the first ever Jedi temple
was pretty much a collection
of **STONE HUTS** on the islands
of Ahch-To. The ancient
buildings have been maintained
over the years by a fussy but
dedicated species known as
the **Caretakers.**

Quietly judging all the
messy visitors

Caretaker

The temple buildings are overlooked by a sprawling uneti tree. This is a **special tree** that communicates with the light side of the Force. Also on the island is a cave full of dark side energy. Because there should always be a **balance between light and dark.** Remember that. It's important.

But don't go in the cave!

A colossal, sprawling tree with surprisingly few leaves

Uneti tree

JEDI HALL OF FAME: YODA

Short in height, but long in years, this 900-year-old was the **Grand Master** of the Jedi Order. He taught younglings and Padawans for over eight centuries. Most went on to do a lot of good.*

*Some did not (see page 40).

Learn to overcome distraction, you must. Provide the distraction, I will.

JEDI HALL OF FAME: QUI-GON JINN

I'm really good at meditation.

Has a reputation for not always following the rules

Philosophical, a **peacekeeper** more than a warrior, and a master at always **keeping his cool...** even when Sith Lords are staring him down. (Which is not easy to do!)

JEDI HALL OF FAME: OBI-WAN KENOBI

My Jedi robes served me well for hermit life.

Doesn't s𝖾𝖾𝗄 adventure but adventure always **finds** him, even when he's retired to hermit life on Tatooine. A **Clone Wars veteran,** Obi-Wan is one of the few Jedi to survive the Jedi Purge. He trained both Anakin Skywalker and Anakin's son Luke in the ways of the Jedi.

JEDI HALL OF FAME: ANAKIN SKYWALKER

Takes charge first, **ASKS QUESTIONS LATER.**
Mechanic, podracer-turned-Jedi-prodigy, ace starfighter
pilot, sand hater. **Don't annoy him** on one
of his bad days.

They say I have
a dark side.

Known for forming
attachments a
little too quickly,
except with his
lightsaber, which
he's always losing.

JEDI HALL OF FAME: MACE WINDU

It's hard to know what's more deadly: the unique **lightsaber style** Mace Windu employs (called Vaapad) or his icy stare. This native of Haruun Kal suffers no fools — so **try not to be one of them.** As a Jedi Master, he leads the Jedi Council while Yoda leads the Jedi Order itself.

> It takes a lot to earn my trust.

Cool purple-bladed lightsaber

JEDI HALL OF FAME: AHSOKA TANO

Sure, I'm young...
go ahead and
underestimate me!

What she lacks in maturity, she makes up for in **ENTHUSIASM.** Anakin Skywalker's Padawan wields **two lightsabers** and enjoys nothing more than slicing her way through sinister battle droids. Ahsoka left the Jedi Order after being **falsely accused** of a crime, but she later became a founding member of the Rebel Alliance.

JEDI HALL OF FAME: LUKE SKYWALKER

Farmboy turned **galactic savior,**[*] Luke helped defeat the Empire. In redeeming his father, Anakin Skywalker (a.k.a. Darth Vader), he showed that it **is** possible to come back from the dark side. And nobody thought it could be done!

[*] Applause.

This is my hero pose.

Green lightsaber to replace blue one he lost

JEDI HALL OF FAME: REY

I've come a long way from Jakku!

She thought she was no one, but the Force had so much more in mind for her. This **scavenger** from Jakku discovered she was so strong in the Force she could perform a **Jedi Mind Trick** without any training and survive a lightsaber duel with Kylo Ren. Is she the last Jedi… or the first of the new?

SO JUST HOW DO THE JEDI TRAVEL FROM THE TEMPLE TO GO ON THEIR IMPORTANT MISSIONS?

Super-fast starships, of course! You'll need **Jedi reflexes** to handle some of them. And don't scratch their paint or dent their hulls or else Master Yoda might tell you off.

Some Jedi starships are unarmed **shuttles,** such as the

T-6 and **Eta,**

useful simply for getting from place to place. These only allow for a couple of passengers. If you want a little more

| legroom, |

the *Consular*-class space cruiser is the vehicle for you.

Consular-Class space cruiser

The Delta-7 *Aethersprite* and Eta-2 *Actis* are not shuttles –
they are Jedi starfighters, speedy one-person attack craft
with enough **armour and weaponry** to go
up against any foe. They need to dock with **hyperspace
rings** in order to travel faster than light, though. So make
sure those rings don't get blown up or you'll be **STRANDED**!

Eta-2 *Actis*-class light
interceptor

Delta-7 *Aethersprite*-
class light interceptor

A Jedi needs to **travel light.** Part of a Jedi's **SELF-DISCIPLINE** (one of the pillars of the Jedi Code, remember?) means they must **be prepared.** No luggage, no hefty backpacks, and no bulky datapad cases. Instead, a Jedi relies on their **utility belt.**

RING RING!

A utility belt can hold a **comlink,** for audio communications, a **holoprojector,** for visual comms, **HOMING BEACONS, rebreathers** for underwater travel, and **many other things.**

Comlink

Holoprojector

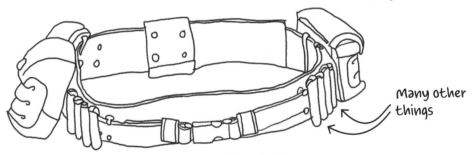

Many other things

Utility belt

From up here, look different, everything does.

Yoda's hover seat

Some equipment is tailored to a particular Jedi, such as **Yoda's hover seat.** Judge him by his size you should not, but sometimes even the **Grand Master** wants to look you in the eye.

Are you a → *WARRIOR*

or a → WORRIER?

We all know that the Jedi are **SUPER COOL GOOD GUYS** with fancy **lightsabers** and some serious duelling **skills.** But did you know, their actual job is to keep the peace?

@?#^%@\#!!!

Translation:
You're doomed!

Unreasonable
bad guy just itching
for a fight

Thanks to their knowledge of the Force, the Jedi have **a pretty good idea** about what's going on in the universe. This gives them a serious advantage when it comes to *negotiating.* Most of the time, they can solve a situation with just their **WORDS** and their **WITS.**

But when words and wits fail (which they sometimes do because hey, let's face it, some bad guys are **SIMPLY. NOT. REASONABLE.** Darth Maul, I'm looking at you!), the Jedi are trained and ready to get those lightsabers out and let the baddies know who's boss!

Hey, let's chill out and talk about this!

Garrrrrrrrr!

Translation: Garrrrrrrrr!

When it comes to **lightsaber duels,** the Jedi are more than prepared, thanks to their YEARS OF TRAINING (and their Force connection, of course!). And no matter how daunting a duel may seem, the Jedi (*almost*) always overcome the challenge, proving their amazing combat abilities.

One-on-one

Count Dooku vs Yoda
Dooku is taller, but Yoda uses whirling, acrobatic jump attacks to make up for his shortness. Yoda saves his Jedi allies, even though Dooku escapes.

Not fair?
Yoda don't care!

Two-on-one

Darth Maul vs Qui-Gon and Obi-Wan
Don't feel sorry for Darth Maul! His double-bladed saberstaff and martial arts moves mean he's more than a match for two Jedi! Qui-Gon is defeated before Obi-Wan finishes off Darth Maul.

Maul will fall!

One-on-four (arms!)

General Grievous vs Obi-Wan
Wielding four lightsabers at once isn't practical - it's simply showing off. But Obi-Wan keeps his cool and aims wisely at Grievous's vulnerable wrists: then only two blades are left, and Obi-Wan emerges victorious.

Four lightsabers are NOT better than one!

Some lightsaber duels pack an **emotional punch,** too. Jedi must be able to **control their feelings** during battle, even when they are surprised, shocked, betrayed, or devastated that everything they've ever thought was a lie.* Don't let the *emotion* of the moment **CLOUD YOUR JUDGMENT.** Stay calm!

* See Vader vs Luke, over there

Yoda vs Palpatine (unexpected Sith Lord)

Grand Master Yoda never even suspected Palpatine was a Sith – until it was too late. Yoda couldn't deflect Palpatine's Force lightning, and Palpatine couldn't defeat his little green foe. Let's call it a tie.

Vader vs Obi–Wan (student vs master)

Obi-Wan always knew he'd have to face his former Padawan in battle again. Luckily the old Jedi had a good trick up his brown sleeves and was able to win and lose at the same time. (More on that on page 85.)

Vader vs Luke (spoiler alert: it's... your... father!)

Mid-battle, Vader drops a bombshell on Luke by revealing he's Luke's father. Luke is understandably distracted, but manages to escape.

The Jedi might be able to control their emotions, but they cannot control the amount of evil in the galaxy. Which means **war is unavoidable.** The Jedi try to keep the peace, but over the years, wars, battles, disputes, and squabbles have occupied **far more time** than the Jedi Order would have liked.

List of war battles, disputes, and squabbles:

THE CLONE WARS

A **strike team** of 200 Jedi went to Geonosis to rescue the captured Obi-Wan, Anakin, and Padmé Amidala. A huge galactic war followed, known as the Clone Wars, and the Jedi became **generals** who led clone trooper battalions into battle.

Around the survivors, a perimeter create!

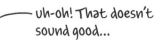

uh-oh! That doesn't sound good...

THE JEDI PURGE

Thanks to a chip implanted in their brains, the **clone troopers** turned on their Jedi leaders and, um, ended their command for good, so to speak. With the **Jedi gone** (some survived but the Order was decimated), Supreme Chancellor Palpatine declared himself

Emperor.

I am declaring myself Emperor.

BIG BAD LASER

Death Star

To **strike fear** into the hearts of everyone in the galaxy he ruled, Emperor Palpatine built a **moon-sized battle station** with a **superlaser** that could destroy an entire planet. People were scared all right!

But after a **daring plan** to steal the Death Star's blueprints, the good old rebels found a **weakness.** And Luke Skywalker proved the Jedi may be down but not out. He flew an X=wing starfighter right along the surface of the Death Star.

Concentrate, Luke!

Luke uses the Force to guide a proton torpedo to the heart of the Death Star.

Luke so believed in **the Force** he even turned off his targeting computer... and got the job done! The Death Star **EXPLODED** and billions of lives across the galaxy were saved. Talk about luck — I mean, amazing Force powers!

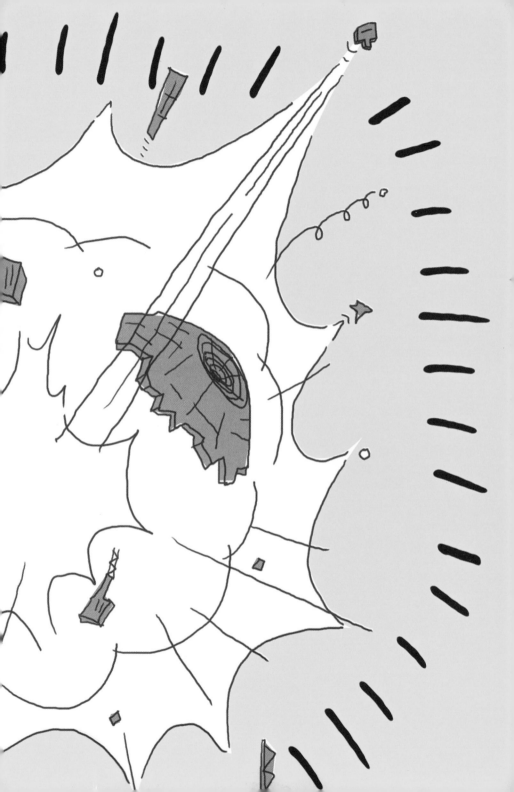

It is **inevitable** that with all these battles and duels, some Jedi end up **sacrificing their lives.** Unlike the Sith, however, who long for **immortality,** the Jedi have a handy way of living on after death. But not just anyone can do it – it is hard! And requires **true commitment** to the Force. (As if it would require anything else…)

So here it is: if a person can **MAINTAIN CONSCIOUSNESS** after death, they could theoretically **live forever.**

It was actually **Qui-Gon Jinn** who discovered this unusual, but rather **useful,** concept.

DING!

Qui-Gon:
always thinking

Qui-Gon understood that the only way a Jedi can achieve eternal life is by **completely** letting go. **Including letting go of their body!**

Whaaaaat?!

Obi-Wan's robes and lightsaber. But no Obi-Wan. Obi-Wan's choice to become a Force ghost gave Vader quite a surprise!

They then become...

ONE with THE FORCE.

As a blue-ish, glowing Force ghost, a Jedi can appear **ANYWHERE** they want and continue to pass on their wisdom. When he became One With the Force, Qui-Gon Jinn led Yoda to a **mysterious** planet where **mysterious** Force Priestesses taught him how **he** could become **One With the Force,** too.

It worked. Decades later, Yoda showed Luke what Force ghosts can do, when he summoned **lightning** to destroy the sacred uneti tree on Ahch-To island. That's powerful!

Shocked face of someone who thought the uneti tree was important.*

*It wasn't.

TRIAL and

TERROR

So you're probably getting by now that being a Jedi is **a pretty cool job.** But it's much **more** than a job. Being a Jedi is a **lifetime commitment.**

Younglings first begin their training in groups, traditionally under the guidance of the Jedi Grand Master himself. A **YOUNGLING** then becomes a **Padawan.**

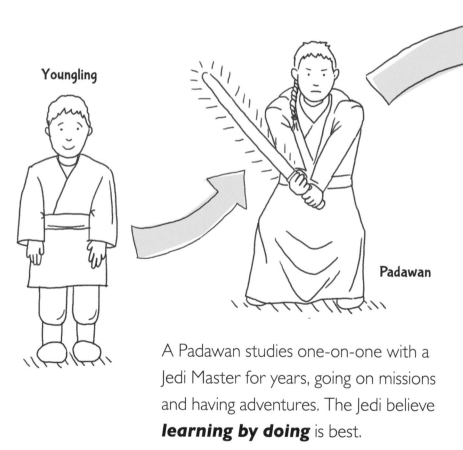

Youngling

Padawan

A Padawan studies one-on-one with a Jedi Master for years, going on missions and having adventures. The Jedi believe **learning by doing** is best.

When they pass the **Jedi Trials,**
Padawans become **Knights.**
Knights carry out a lot of the
Jedi Order's business.

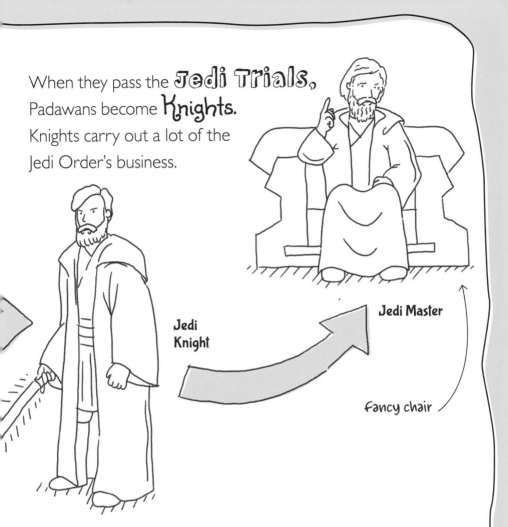

Jedi
Knight

Jedi Master

fancy chair

Because of this, some Jedi Knights **DON'T HAVE TIME**
to train a Padawan of their own.

But those who do, and whose Padawan becomes a Knight
themselves, are then **_upgraded_** to the rank of **MASTER.**
Some Masters get to sit (literally, they get a fancy chair)
on the **Jedi Council.**

You might be wondering, **how, exactly,** does someone become **Force-sensitive?**

There's a simple answer, which some people will find exciting, while others will be disappointed: **you don't have to do anything.** That's right. Force sensitivity is something you are born with – or **NOT** born with.

Sometimes, Force sensitivity **runs in families,** but every so often it will **pop up** from absolutely nowhere. This can be quite surprising for everyone involved.

The Jedi like to recruit younglings when they're **very young** (we're talking cute little Force-sensitive toddlers here). This way, the recruits grow up **immersed** in Jedi life.

He's too old!

But I'm only 10!

Yoda (900 years old)

Anakin Skywalker

Some Force-sensitive kids escape notice, though. If, say, they grow up **totally oblivious** on a far-flung Outer Rim world, they may have to do something **spectacular** to gain a Jedi's attention. Like winning a podrace, for example.

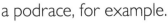

Getting discovered for your Force sensitivity is the **easy** part! Once a youngling has been selected, they move to the **Jedi Temple** on Coruscant and begin their training. (Remember that?)

Fun, yes.
Hard work, ~~double~~ triple yes.

Jedi training mostly means a LOT of
classes!

And even more
homework.

And even more
practising.

Lightsaber Basics

Defence Against the Dark Side

Mind Tricks for DUMMIES

THE JEDI

Where There's a Whill There's a Way

The Force Whisperer

LIGHT SIDE RULEBOOK

But all that time with the books is **WORTH IT** because younglings get to do something that can only be described as fun, awesome, and **Super cool:** **lightsaber classes** led by Yoda himself.

Um... great...

Jedi younglings are taught by the **best of the best.**
Each day, experienced Jedi Masters teach at the Jedi Temple.

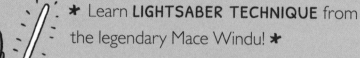

* Learn **LIGHTSABER TECHNIQUE** from the legendary Mace Windu! *

* Find out which planets have **breathable air** from Plo Koon! *

* Tour the Jedi Archives with Jocasta Nu! *

* Discover the best way to **survive on bugs** and swamp plants from Yoda! *

As dangerous as a gundark's nest, politics is.

Sith holocron

Jedi Master
Luminara Unduli:
holocron expert

Jedi
holocron

**Sith holocron
= bad.**

**Jedi holocron
= good.**

Show and tell sessions might include **rare Jedi artefacts** – and sometimes even Sith ones.

Younglings especially look forward to their **field trips.** They get to learn about life **OUTSIDE** the Temple in the company of well-travelled Jedi Knights, droids, and holographic tour guides.

Once they've proven they're **mature** enough to handle a

LIGHTSABER,

younglings build their own and **PERSONALISE** it.

Imagine their excitement: They get to choose the colour and shape of the **hilt** and learn how all the parts fit together. The colour of the blade comes from the precious KYBER CRYSTAL that lies at the heart of each lightsaber. There's **only one** kyber crystal that's meant for any one Jedi, so every lightsaber is **completely unique.**

Building a lightsaber hilt

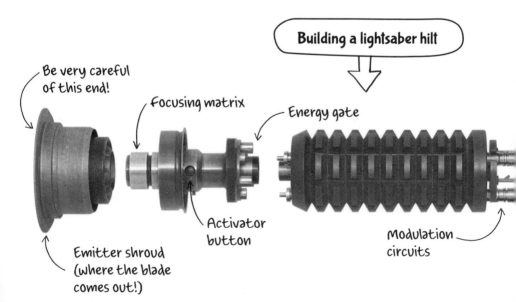

Be very careful of this end!

Focusing matrix

Energy gate

Activator button

Emitter shroud (where the blade comes out!)

Modulation circuits

First things first, though: younglings need to **FIND** their kyber crystal. To do this, they journey into the **dark** and **mysterious**

crystal cave.

Then, they must navigate through the cave (which is filled with Force energy) and find the crystal that **CALLS OUT** to them. Let's hope it's not a red one!

Hello, my sparkly little friend.

Power cell

Belt ring

Kyber crystal

Handgrip ridges

There's **not much point** in building a lightsaber if you don't know how to use it. So younglings begin their **lightsaber training.** There are lots of techniques to learn: different **STANCES,** offensive and defensive **moves,** different **combat forms,** and of course, the **BASICS** – like how to turn the blade on and off.

Lightsaber up in front of you

Deflecting attacks back at your enemies defeats them with their own aggression.

Lightsaber held out to the side

A calm opening pose that can become either an offensive or defensive move.

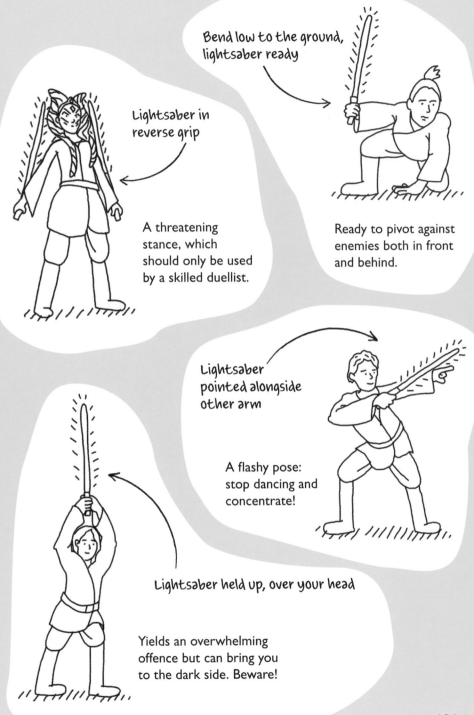

Bend low to the ground, lightsaber ready

Ready to pivot against enemies both in front and behind.

Lightsaber in reverse grip

A threatening stance, which should only be used by a skilled duellist.

Lightsaber pointed alongside other arm

A flashy pose: stop dancing and concentrate!

Lightsaber held up, over your head

Yields an overwhelming offence but can bring you to the dark side. Beware!

Most of the time, Jedi will **choose their own Padawan** from the Temple's class of younglings. (Sometimes, the Council may choose to **assign a Padawan** to a particular Knight.)

So what makes a Jedi choose a **specific** Padawan?

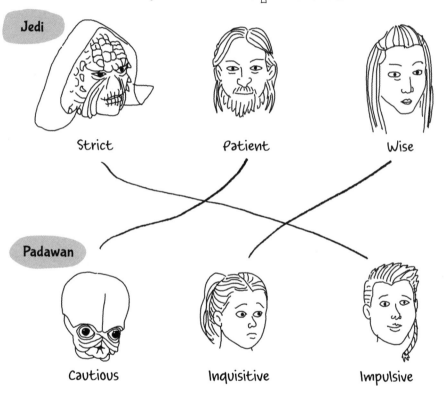

Jedi

Strict   Patient   Wise

Padawan

Cautious   Inquisitive   Impulsive

Maybe it's a **SPECIAL SKILL** a certain youngling has mastered. Or they demonstrated **bravery or kindness**. Or there's something about the **personality** of a particular youngling that a Knight feels is a **good fit** with their own.

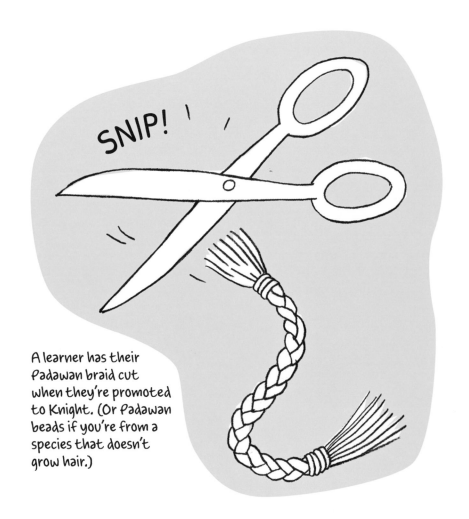

SNIP!

A learner has their Padawan braid cut when they're promoted to Knight. (Or Padawan beads if you're from a species that doesn't grow hair.)

Other times, **galactic events** may shape the trial. For many Padawans, the Clone Wars represented the ultimate trial, as they were forced to become commanders of clone trooper units. Taking on the **responsibility** of a military leadership role may be almost as **daunting** as facing up to an evil Sith who happens to be your dad. *Almost.*

Of course, some Jedi didn't spend their **early years** training at the Jedi Temple on Coruscant. They learned their 𝕁𝕖𝕕𝕚 𝕤𝕜𝕚𝕝𝕝𝕤 in a **different way.**

EZRA BRIDGER

Ezra was just a regular, Force-sensitive kid surviving on the mean streets of the planet Lothal. But then he was trained as a Jedi by Kanan Jarrus, and joined a crew of rebels aboard a ship called the Ghost.

LUKE SKYWALKER

Luke grew up on a moisture farm. (B-O-R-I-N-G!) When he found out his dad was a famous Jedi, he went to find the legendary Yoda. Yoda was hiding on a swampy planet called Dagobah, but he agreed to train Luke. Phew!

KYLO REN

The son of Princess Leia and Han Solo, of course Kylo Ren was going to train as a Jedi! He was taught by Luke, but then became **obsessed** with the legacy of his grandpa (Darth Vader), so he turned to the dark side. His next master was a scary guy called Snoke.

REY

Rey was busy being a simple scavenger when she discovered a powerful power inside her. She eventually tracked down Luke who was hiding out on the island of Ahch-To. She convinced him to train her. (It wasn't easy!)

When a Jedi becomes a Knight, the **greatest** thing they can do is **pass on** all they have learnt.*

By being a **mentor and role model,** a Jedi ensures that the next generation of Padawans and Jedi will carry on the Order's **ancient traditions.**

*And also keep the galaxy peaceful and safe.

But passing the torch is a **BIG RESPONSIBILITY** – especially if that torch is a lightsaber! You must take this responsibility **seriously.**

Sometimes a Jedi will go the **extra mile** for their Padawan, like continuing with lessons even as a Force ghost. Talk about **dedication!** Keeping up with lesson plans even after becoming One With the Force just might make you *Jedi **Teacher of the Year.***

Train yourself to let go of everything you fear to lose.

HOMEWORK:
What do you fear to lose and why?

I fear to lose my body. See-through is just not a good look!

When the Jedi Order fell (Emperor Palpatine's **terrible** plan, the Jedi Purge, remember?), the galaxy was **plunged into darkness.** And **THE LIGHT** is only just starting to return after brave farmboy, and super Jedi, **Luke Skywalker,** helped defeat **the Empire.** The nasty Emperor also died. Hooray! (Well, we'll see…)

So now, there are only a few Jedi left, some **in hiding,** some **unaware** of their Force powers, some aware but with **no one to teach them.**

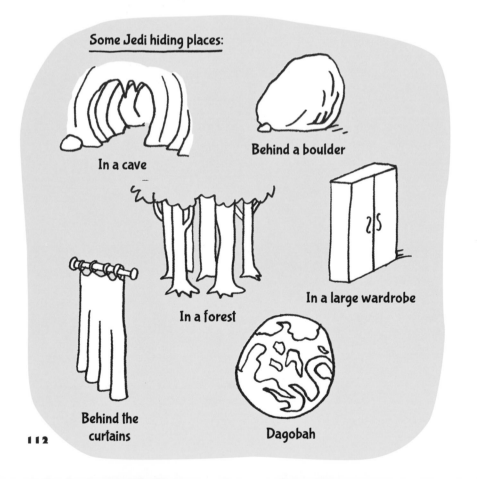

Some Jedi hiding places:

In a cave

Behind a boulder

In a forest

In a large wardrobe

Behind the curtains

Dagobah

The fact that there are so few Jedi means that the galaxy needs them oh-so-much more. But there won't be an **awesome Jedi comeback** if the First Order has anything to say about it. The First Order **(Booo!)** is a tyrannical regime determined to finish what the Empire started… and **WIPE OUT THE JEDI** once and for **all.** (If its leaders can stop squabbling and focus on the job at hand.)

General Hux

Supreme
Leader Snoke

Kylo Ren

But he's not really! **113**

With these **dark side baddies** running the First Order and hunting down Jedi, the Force is as unbalanced as ever.

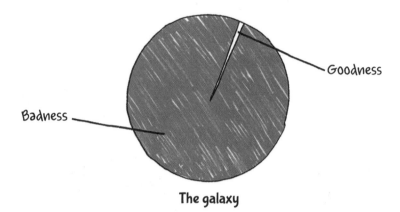

Goodness

Badness

The galaxy

Darth Vader's grandson, Ben Solo, turned to the ᗪᗩᖇᛕ ᔕᛁᗪᗴ and gave himself the scary-sounding name, **KYLO REN.** A ᔕymᛒoᒪ oᖴ ᖴᗴᗩᖇ is exactly what he wants to be, too. He doesn't even **need** to wear his mask to keep himself alive, like his grandad did – he wears it to **PAY TRIBUTE** to Vader and **terrorise** his enemies.

Strong in the Force but unfortunately lacking in control. (Not a good combination.)

Under my helmet I look quite normal actually...

Kylo Ren

Known to use Force
lightning in fits of anger ⟶

Supreme Leader Snoke

A mysterious, powerful (and not-so-nice-to-look-at) **Force user** from the Unknown Regions **corrupts** Ben Solo from afar. Snoke's **telekinetic** and **mind-probing** abilities are profound. That is, until he is cut down by Kylo Ren. So much for him...

Are you saying
that I don't
look normal?

Kylo Ren and Snoke **aren't Sith**, but those sneaky Sith might not be gone after all... Palpatine has been brought **back from the dead** and is hanging out in secret on a Sith planet named Exegol. He been pulling Snoke's and the **First Order's strings** from behind the scenes!

Known for being
a real meddler

Spoilers, I
MADE Snoke!

Darth Sidious/ Sheev
Palpatine / Emperor
returned once more

We've met **Rey** before, but she's very **relevant** to the story now, so let's learn more about her. Rey grew up on a sandy planet called Jakku where **nothing exciting ever happened.**
(Well, there was a big battle once, a long time ago.)

Nothing to see here...

Or here...

Rey was raised hearing **stories** about the Jedi. And now she's living in one. She never realised she had **Force powers** of her own.

But when Kylo Ren probed her mind with **the Force,** Rey discovered her own powers and pushed back. She was able to use a **Jedi Mind Trick** on a stormtrooper after just a few minutes. Pretty impressive!

You will remove these restraints. And leave this cell, with the door open.

I will remove those restraints. And leave this cell, with the door open.

And then you will get me a sandwich — a cheese one, with a pickle.

And then I will get you a sandwich — a cheese one, with a pickle.

Later, Rey found she had a natural affinity for **LIGHTSABER COMBAT** — much to Kylo Ren's dismay. Rey also has incredibly **fast reflexes.** She can **leap** over a speeding TIE fighter, and even pilot the *MILLENNIUM FALCON,* which is notoriously tricky.

Rey even seems to have **unlocked** a new Force power. Rey and Kylo Ren can open a mysterious **Force connection** with each other's minds and even physically interact. This greatly **disturbs** both of them.

Why are **YOU** here?

Why are you **HERE?!**

Rey and Kylo Ren's strong **Force connection** is **troubling** for both of them. What does it mean?

Er...

Rey continues to study and grow in her **FORCE POWERS.** Can she **harness them** to take on Kylo and the First Order? What does the future – and the Force – have in store for her?

Don't mess
with her →

119

With all her powers, Rey really needed a **Jedi** to GUIDE her. Luckily, she was able to track down the **very elusive**

Luke Skywalker.

Under Luke's guidance, Rey **mastered** her Jedi skills. She was also taught to **learn from the mistakes** of all the Jedi who came before her.

The greatest teacher, failure is.

Yoda, full of cheery advice

This is when **PALPATINE** decided to reveal himself to the whole galaxy. Those Sith sure know how to plan a comeback.

Long have I waited...

REY isn't happy about this at all, so she goes on a **quest** with her pals to find and defeat him.

On the way, she finds out that the evil Palpatine is her **grandfather** (GASP!) and, with Leia's help, **redeems** Kylo, who now calls himself **BEN SOLO** again.

My name is Ben Solo.

Rey feels a *little glum* about being the grandaughter of the **biggest baddie ever,** but a ghostly Luke (one with the Force now) turns up to give her a much-needed **PEP TALK.** Feeling **much better,** Rey zips off to planet **Exegol** for a long-overdue **FAMILY REUNION.**

With Ben's help and some familiar Jedi voices, Rey defeats her **grumpy grandad,** for ever this time, in front of an audience of thousands of creepy **SITH** fans:

Terry, can you see what's going on?

Not a clue, Linda.

Well it isn't sounding good...

Thanks to her **FORCE POWERS,** Rey has **saved the entire galaxy** (Jedi to-do list complete). Sadly, Ben doesn't make it, but he too finds peace with the mysterious Force.

Re-uniting with her pals, Rey has a **big party** to celebrate that the Sith are **FINALLY GONE.** They deserve it.

The galaxy is at peace once more!

So go: Find your **happy place** – your own remote island or swamp planet – where you can meditate on what's *important* to you. **Reflect** on all you have discovered here about the Jedi and the Force. **Learn** from past mistakes and **look toward** to a Sith-free future.

Hopefully what you learn will **LIGHT YOUR PATH** through galaxies near… and far, far away.

The end.

Rey's pal BB-8

Glossary

ACCUMULATED
Gathered together.

AFFINITY
A natural understanding of, or ability to do, something.

ARCHIVE
Library or collection of historical information.

ARTEFACT
Object with historical or cultural interest.

CANTINA
A bar where outlaws and criminals tend to hang out.

Not for kids!

CLONE WARS
A series of galaxy-wide battles fought between the Republic and those who wished to break away from it.

CONJURE
Create.

CONSCIOUSNESS
Being aware of what's happening.

COSMIC FORCE
The Force that connects everything in the galaxy. It gets its energy from the Living Force.

DAUNTING
Intimidating or hard to deal with.

DEVOTEE
A strong believer.

ELUSIVE
Difficult to find.

ENHANCED
Made better.

That doesn't sound good!

EMPIRE
A tyrannical power that rules the galaxy under the leadership of Emperor Palpatine, a Sith Lord.

EXILE
Unable to return to your planet, country, or home.

FORCE LIGHTNING
Scary Force energy shot out from a villain's fingertips.

HERMIT
Someone who lives all alone.

HILT
Handle of a weapon.

HOMING BEACON
A device that is hidden on a vehicle or person that allows its user to track it.

IMMORTALITY
Being able to live forever.

JEDI MIND TRICK
A way Jedi can make weak-minded people obey them.

JEDI PURGE
The attempt by Chancellor Palpatine to destroy the entire Jedi Order.

SO mean!

KYBER CRYSTAL
A very powerful crystal
used in lightsabers.

LEGACY
What a person leaves behind
after they are gone.

LIVING FORCE
Energy that is created
from all living beings.

LUMINOUS
Something that gives off light.

MANTRA
A statement.

MENTOR
A teacher or advisor.   Gotta get one
of these!

MOISTURE FARM
A farm on hot planets that
collects moisture from the air.

NEGOTIATE
To reach a solution
through discussion.

OPTIMISM
Being positive about
what will happen.

PARSEC
A unit of distance.

PODRACER
A fast vehicle that is raced in the
sport known as podracing.

PORTAL
A doorway or entrance.

POTENTIAL
A person's skills and
qualities, that can
be improved in the future.

REBEL
Someone who is fighting
against the evil Empire.

REBEL ALLIANCE
The organisation that resists
and fights against the Empire.

REDEEMING
Saving someone who
has done bad things.

REPUBLIC
The fair, democratic government
that rules most planets in the
galaxy.

SCAVENGER
Someone who collects junk. ←

SENATE   One person's junk
The government   is another person's
of the Republic.   treasure...

TELEKINETIC
Able to move things
with one's mind.

TREATY
An agreement.

VAAPAD
A very fierce form
of lightsaber combat.

VETERAN
Someone who used
to fight in an army.

Index

Ahch-To (mysterious, spiritual planet) 56–59, 87

BB-8 123

Bridger, Ezra (Jedi Rebel) 106

Chosen One, the (an ancient prophecy) 42–45

clone troopers
fighting alongside the Jedi 78, 105
gone bad 41, 79

Clone Wars (a trap!) 41, 78, 105

comlink 22, 70

Cosmic Force, the 46

Death Star, before and after it's blown up 80–83

Dooku, Count (Jedi-turned-Sith) 40, 74

Emperor, the 39, 44, 52, 79, 112, 115 see also Palpatine; Sidious, Darth

First Order, the 112, 114, 118

Force, the 23, 26–27, 31, 46, 81
being One with the Force (when you're dead) 84–87, 109
dark side (remember: BAD!) 29, 30, 36–39, 66, 101, 115
keeping it balanced 14, 16, 43–45, 47, 59, 114
the light side (remember: GOOD!) 24, 28, 30, 32–35, 41
and Jedi turning to the dark side 38, 40, 107, 114

Force ghosts 85–87, 109

Force powers 93, 115, 116, 118
Force connections 118
Force lightning 39, 76, 87, 115
mind probing 115, 116
mind tricks 27, 67, 116–117
reflexes 27, 68, 117
sensing things 27, 81
telekinesis 27, 115

Force sensitives 13, 27, 43, 92–3

Force-Wielders (The Father, The Daughter, and The Son) 47

Grand Master 51, 60, 71, 90 see also Yoda

Grievous, General 75

holocrons (glowing memory cubes) 55, 97

holoprojector 70

Jedi Archives (So. Much. Data) 54–55, 96

Jedi Code (it's not all just blowing stuff up) 31, 33, 70

Jedi Council, a.k.a. the Jedi High Council 50–51, 64, 91, 102

Jedi Order 10–11, 24–25, 31, 53, 112

Jedi Purge 62, 79, 112

Jedi Temple
the massive one on Coruscant 51–55, 94, 96
the one on a Force portal on Lothal 46
the ancient one on Ahch-To 56–59
Vader's one on Mustafar 46

Jedi Trials 91, 104–5

Jinn, Qui-Gon 61
spotting Anakin's potential 14–16
dying and coming back as a Force-ghost 75, 84–6

Kenobi, Obi-Wan 62, 78, 85, 103
cool dueler 75, 77

kyber crystals (sparkly!) 98, 99

lightsabers 22
build your own! 98–99
in combat 64, 73, 100–101, 117
in duels 67, 74–77

learning to use them (steady, now!)
19, 95, 96, 100–101
more than one at once 65, 75
purple 64
Living Force, the 46
Maul, Darth (dangerous Sith) 38–39,
75
Nu, Jocasta (Jedi librarian) 54, 96
Padawans (still not a Jedi yet) 11,
90–91, 102–103, 104–105, 108–109
Palpatine 39 *see also* Emperor, the
dueling Yoda with Force lightning
76
and his sneaky plans 41, 76, 79, 80,
112, 120–121
Prime Jedi, the (the very first Jedi)
56–57
Ren, Kylo 107, 121
taking a fancy to the dark side
38, 40, 107, 113, 114–115
and his weird connection with
Rey 67, 116–118, 121
Rey 67, 107, 116–122, 123
Sidious, Darth 41 *see also* Emperor,
the; Palpatine
Skywalker, Anakin
is he the Chosen One? 14–16,
43–44
his good-old Jedi days 62, 63, 78, 93
and his journey to the dark side
38, 43–44, 66 *see also* Vader, Darth
Skywalker, Luke 56, 66
blowing up the Death Star 81
duelling his own father 77
as a student 13, 62, 87, 106
as a teacher 107, 120
Snoke, why you shouldn't mess with
him 38, 107, 113, 115
starships 68–69

Tano, Ahsoka 65, 104
training to be Jedi 13, 18–19, 90–91,
gruelling trials 91, 104–105
as a youngling 90, 94–97, 98–99,
100–101
as a Padawan 90–91, 102–103,
104–105, 108–109
unconventional routes 14–16, 67, 106,
107
Unduli, Luminara (Jedi Master) 97
uneti tree 59, 87
utility belt 22, 70
Vader, Darth 77, 85
see also Skywalker, Anakin
as a dad 66, 77
as a granddad 107, 114
loving the dark side 38, 40, 43–44, 46
Windu, Mace (Jedi Master) 51, 64, 96
X-wing starfighter 81
Yoda 60, 86–87
an awesome dueler 74, 76
as Grand Master 51, 60, 71
as a teacher 40, 60, 93, 95, 96,
106, 120
younglings (the littlest Jedi kids)
how they're selected 13, 93
how they're trained 14, 19, 90,
94–97, 98–99, 100–101, 102–103
and lightsabers 98–99, 100–101

Project Editor Shari Last
Senior Editor Emma Grange
Project Art Editor Jon Hall
Senior Designer Nathan Martin
Managing Editor Sarah Harland
Managing Art Editor Vicky Short
Senior Pre-Production Producer Jennifer Murray
Senior Producers Mary Slater and Louise Daly
Publisher Julie Ferris
Art Director Lisa Lanzarini
Publishing Director Mark Searle

Illustrations by Dan Crisp and Jon Hall

DK would like to thank Matt Jones and Megan Douglass
for editorial help and Elizabeth Dowsett for the index.

First published in Great Britain in 2020
by Dorling Kindersley Limited
80 Strand, London WC2R 0RL
A Penguin Random House Company

10 9 8 7 6 5 4 3 2 1
001–316370–May/2020

A CIP catalogue record for this book is
available from the British Library.
ISBN 978-0-24140-918-3

Printed and bound in China

A WORLD OF IDEAS:
SEE ALL THERE IS TO KNOW

www.dk.com

www.starwars.com